THE GODS AND MEN OF ARGORON

The Gods and Men of Argoron is a work of fiction. References to real people, events, establishments, organizations, or locales are intended only to provide the sense of authenticity and are use fictitiously. All other characters, all incidents, dialogue are drawn from the author's imagination and are not to be seen as real.

Copyright © 2022. All rights reserved.

Published by Dark Titan Publishing. A division of Dark Titan Entertainment.

Prodigious Worlds is an imprint of Dark Titan Entertainment.

Paperback ISBN: 979-8-9866393-9-0
eBook ISBN: 979-8-2180973-0-1

darktitanentertainment.com

WORKS BY TY'RON W. C. ROBINSON II

BOOKS/SHORT STORIES

DARK TITAN UNIVERSE SAGA

MAIN SERIES
Dark Titan Knights
The Resistance Protocol
Tales of the Scattered
Tales of the Numinous
Day of Octagon
Crossbreed
Heaven's Called
The Oranos Imperative
Underworld
Magicks & Mysticism

SPIN-OFFS
In A Glass of Dawn: The Casebook of Travis Vail
Maveth: Bloodsport
The Curse of The Mutant-Thing
Trail of Vengeance
War of The Thunder Gods

ONE-SHOTS
Maveth, The Death-Bringer Mystery of The Mutant-Thing Shade & Switchblade
Retribution of Cain
The Mythologists
Ambush Bot
Kang-Zhu
Cheeseburger Man
Tessa Balthazar
Elite 5

COLLECTIONS
Dark Titan Omnibus: Volume 1
Dark Titan Omnibus: Volume 2
Dark Titan One-Shot Collection
Dark Titan One-Shot Collection II

THE HAUNTED CITY SAGA
The Legendary Warslinger: The Haunted City I
Battle of Astolat: A Haunted City Prequel (KOBO Exclusive)
Redemption of the Lost: The Haunted City II
Helper's Hand: A Haunted City One-Shot
The Haunted City Collection

SYMBOLUM VENATORES
Symbolum Venatores: The Gabriel Kane Collection
Hod: A Symbolum Venatores Book
Symbolum Venatores: War of The Two Kingdoms Symbolum Venatores: Elrad's Chronicles
Symbolum Venatores Collection

EVERWAR UNIVERSE
EverWar Universe: Knights & Lords
Avior vs. Dekar

PRODIGIOUS WORLDS
Mark Porter of Argoron
Raiders of Vanok
Praxus of Lithonia
Prodigious Worlds: The First Worlds
The Sword of Praxus

FRIGHTENED! SERIES
Frightened!: The Beginning

INSTINCTS SERIES
Lost in Shadows: Remastered
Instincts Point Hope
The New Haven/Point Hope Incidens

THE HORDE TRILOGY
The Horde
The Dreaded Ones

DARK TITAN'S THE DEAD DAYS
Accounts of The Dead Days

OTHER BOOKS
The Book of The Elect
The Extended Age Omnibus
The Eleventh Hour: A Chevah Mythos Story
The Supreme Pursuer: Darkness of the Hunt
Massacre in the Dusk
Venture into Horror: Tales of the Supernatural
The Universe of Realms Omnibus: Book 1
The Universe of Realms Omnibus: Book 2

THE DARK TITAN AUDIO EXPERIENCE PODCAST
Season 1: Introductions
Season 2: In a Glass of Dawn
Season 2.5: Accounts of The Dead Days
Season 3: Battle For Astolat
Season 4: Hallow Sword: Cursed

THE GODS AND MEN OF ARGORON

TY'RON W. C. ROBINSON II

CONTENTS

CHAPTER 1: WE EXIST
1

CHAPTER 2: THE GOD OF DESTRUCTION
3

CHAPTER 3: THE HASTY SPIRIT
8

CHAPTER 4: A WONDER TO GAZE UPON A GOD
14

CHAPTER 5: THE HIBARIAN FOREST
23

CHAPTER 6: THE WAY FORWARD
31

CHAPTER 7: SUMMONING THE GOD
34

CHAPTER 8: BETWEEN GODS AND MEN
38

CHAPTER 1: WE EXIST

Mark Porter of Earth stared at the living light which was present before him.

"You are what?" Porter asked again.

"You heard what I said. I am a God of Argoron."

"Sorry. But I'm not familiar with the gods of this planet. I just came here not long ago."

"I know. I know."

"You know?"

"I saw the portal which brought you to this planet. I am aware of your homeworld. Your kind call it Earth, yes?"

"We do. How do you know of Earth?"

"Again. I am a God of Argoron. We know many things."

Porter moved around the area, his eyes locked on the light entity.

"Tell me this. What kind of god are you?"

"What do you mean?"

"What are you the god of?"

"If I would tell you, you would not be pleased nor calm."

"You're an evil one?"

"Evil? No, Earthman. I am a savior. A savior to this planet and its inhabitations. Yet, they refuse to hear my words. My guidelines for peace."

"Then appear before them reasonably and maybe they'll give you an ear to hear."

The light flickered as the sound of a door creaked open. Porter turned and saw Princess Lola Arribel approaching him, still covered in her white sleeping robe from the shoulders down to her feet. He quickly returned his sight toward the light entity, only to find the light dimmed and gone.

"Porter. What are you doing out here?"

"I came to get some air and there was, there was some king of being made of light."

"A being made of light?"

"Yes. It told me it was a god of this planet."

Lola paused. With a gentle nod, she returned inside and Porter followed.

CHAPTER 2: THE GOD OF DESTRUCTION

The following morning as the sun had risen over the city of Taranopolis, Porter followed Lola through the palace as she brought him into a room. The room only known as the Histories of Argoron. A room covered with shelves full of scrolls and books. Categories were centered upon the floors near the shelves. Porter had never seen the room and was astonished as to how many works were placed within such a place. He questioned if the people of the city were aware of the library and the knowledge it contains. Lola only responded with a slow voice, stating the people of the city had given the King the scrolls and books. From every corner of Argoron. From neighboring cities and kingdoms tot faraway lands not seen in ages. Lola walked by shelf after shelf. Her eyes fixated on a certain categories and after three more steps, she found it.

"What have you found?" Porter questioned.

"This. The category of the religions of this planet."

"Religions? They have religions here?"

"Religions are on every planet if you know where to look."

Lola searched the middle shelf and read the spines of the books and the initials upon the scrolls. Finding one book labeled the "Ancient Argoronian Texts", she grabbed it and went to the nearby table. Sitting down as the book opened. She asked Porter to describe what he saw and he said the same as before. The light entity. Never speaking its name and offering new knowledge to a newcomer of the planet. Even calling itself a savior.

The pages turned and turned and on one page was an image of a light entity. Porter stopped Lola's page-turning, placing his finger on the image.

"That's it."

Lola looked and read the details of the page. Porter could not because he's yet to read Argoronian language. Lola stood up as she continued to read the page as Porter asked what it says. Lola sighed, placing the book down on the table.

"It's not good."

"Tell me." Porter said. "What isn't good?"

"The page states the god you encountered is named *Omnicron*."

"Omnicron. Ok. What about him? Is he everything he told me or not?"

"The ancients referred to him as the God of Destruction."

Porter took a pause.

"He only told me he was a savior. That he could bring peace to the planet and end all the conflicts thereof."

"That's the thing. He gives false promises, only to bring desolation to wherever he's seen.

"And you believe since he's made himself known, he's about to bring destruction upon your father's kingdom?"

"Precisely. Why else would he appear? And to someone who's new to these things."

"Fair point. Now, the question we both must know is how do we find him."

"What do you mean find him?"

"We find him. Confront him and end his ploys upon this planet for good."

"Mark, he's a god."

"What is that supposed to mean?"

"You can't be serious. We don't have the manpower to challenge a god."

"We won't know until we take our shot. Now, he appeared to me last night and I would not be surprised if he were to do it again."

"I take it you've never faced a god before. Aren't there gods back on your world?"

"There are. But, most haven't seen them in ages if ever."

Lola sighed, walking over to place the book back on the shelf. Once they prepared to leave the library, King R'akl stood at the door. His hands behind his back and his expression still. Seeing him, they both bowed.

"Father. I didn't know you were present."

"I just arrived, daughter. No need to continue speaking with your heads low. Rise up."

Both had risen and greeted the King. He questioned their purpose within the library. Lola showed him the book and the look on his face, a curious one brought forth a question. Lola explained to him of Porter's encounter the night before and R'akl shook his head. A slight bow had followed as he held the book in his hand.

"This is not the first time he has been seen in this city."

"What do you mean?" Porter asked. "Are there others who have saw him here?"

"Several. Most refuse to come to the truth of the matter. One witness told me what he saw. The same thing you saw last night. It is Omnicron. The God of Destruction. N the ancient days of this planet, Omnicron was known to destroy cities, villages, and towns. Kingdoms and empires of our world either fell before him or worshipped him to be spared. Such is his nature and now, he has come to bring much trouble to this city and most certainly to the people of this planet once again. All during my reign."

"Then why make himself known to me? I'm not from this world."

"That is the clear reason for his decision. If he appeared before a native to this planet, they would've known something strange. It wouldn't take them long to figure out the visitor of light."

Lola reached for the book as her father held it back. A sigh exhaled from his mouth with a look of light disappointment. R'akl nodded and handed her the book, commanding her to return it to the shelf.

"What's our next move?" Porter questioned.

"We prepare ourselves and this city for Omnicron's ongoing plot. I'm not certain how we can battle a god and win."

"There's always a way."

Lola returned to Porter and her father. The three began to think of ways to face Omnicron as they knew it wouldn't be long before he's sighted once more.

Elsewhere in the vast deserts of Argoron, an army of rebels clothed in their blood-red armor, nearly blended in with the sands beneath their feet. They sat in a camp. Dozens of soldiers walked through carrying swords, shields, and spears. In the largest tent, sitting at his desk was none other than Saban Jai. The former lieutenant of King R'akl's army and the original proposal to marry Princess Lola. Saban sat at the desk, readying a scroll sent from a fellow ally concerning the changes that have occurred in recent days after the battle. Entering the tent was another of Saban's allies.

"Ivo Rankez." Saban said, standing up. "You've arrived."

"I received news of your need. I have come to aid my effort in this fight."

"I thank you well, friend. We must gather enough forces to

eliminate R'akl's own soldiers and his newfound lieutenant."

"The Earthman." Ivo said. "Yes. He's a keen one indeed. He managed to slay the Wyvern King. With his own power."

"I know. There's something about him that makes him almost superior to us. Is it because he's from another world or is there something the gods are plotting to our ignorance?"

"The gods are on our side, Saban." Ivo grinned. "Trust the process."

Saban nodded and glanced down at the map on the desk. Ivo took a look and saw the details for a small, planned attack on Taranopolis. A larger smile formed upon Ivo's face as he turned toward Saban.

"This small attack? How soon is it?"

"Close. Although, I will not be able to attend. There are still some matters to focus on before I return to that city."

"Let me lead a small garrison into the city. Cause a bit of trouble. That way, I can see how strong R'akl's forces are and see truly what this Earthman is capable of."

"Are you prepared for such a task?"

"I've done my shares of battles in the past and I was once the dungeon keeper for the kingdom. I have my ways."

Saban nodded.

"Very well. Gather which men will suit you for the cause and once you have them at your number, you may go and see what they're capable of."

"As you say." Ivo bowed and exited the tent with haste.

CHAPTER 3: THE HASTY SPIRIT

It was within no time, Ivo arrived in the streets of Taranopolis with his garrison behind him. Standing firm in their place, Ivo's stare brought terror upon the civilians as he began to walk toward the palace, yelling out R'akl's name. From the palace doors, Porter and Lola walked out, seeing Ivo in the distance with his armed men standing behind him.

"The scientist." Lola said.

"I remember him." Porter added. "He was there when I first came here. Inside the prison walls."

"He was notorious for dwelling down there. Believing he could help those in need."

R'akl stepped out from behind his daughter and Porter as he was focused on Ivo. A disappointed nod he expressed only to see Ivo's grin. Lola wondered what should they do and R'akl did not back down. He walked toward Ivo and stood within several feet from him and his army.

"Why have you returned?"

"To make a statement!" Ivo yelled. "What happened in the last battle was only a mishap. What will happen this day shall be remembered for the ages."

R'akl looked out toward Ivo's men. Counting them within his mind. He smirked and cocked his head.

"It appears you do not have the manpower to take this city nor this kingdom from my hands."

"The number does not matter. What does is the sheer determination I have brought before you."

"Where's Saban Jai?"

"He's busy with other matters. Sent me here to finish the job."

"Are you sure you want another battle, Rankez? Another loss under your belt?"

"I will not lose this day. Only succeed."

R'akl knew within that Ivo would not surrender. It was never within him to make such a choice. From there, the King turned and walked back over to his daughter and Porter. He looked the Earthman in the eyes and Porter knew what he must do. The three returned inside the palace to the laughter of Ivo and his men following them. However, their laughter was cut short with the arrival of R'akl's soldiers. Over three dozen of them armed and ready for the fight. Walking through them was Porter. Clothed in new armor, shining of gold and in his right hand was his sword. The same he used in the gladiatorial arena. wrapped on his left forearm was the chain and the large, sharpened blade attached to it hung below. Ivo glared up toward the palace balcony and saw R'akl standing over.

"I will give you one last chance to surrender and turn away, Rankez!" R'akl spoke.

Ivo grunted and slammed his sword into the rocky ground. He pointed upward with anger in his eyes.

"I will never surrender! Never!"

"Very well. Let the battle commence!"

The armies ran toward each other as the civilians made their way to escape the area. Lola remained with her father, standing beside him on the balcony. Ivo's soldiers clashed with R'akl's and the battle intensified. Spears clashed against shields as if thunder itself cracked from the heavens and spoke with a loud voice. Swords swiped against another like the ringing echoes of an anvil at work. Through the battle, Porter moved with speed. A speed unlike anything seen in Argoron. His sword slaughtered many soldiers as did his chain-blade. Tossing it into the backs of soldiers and pulling them toward him, only to impale them with his sword.

"What has become of him?" Ivo asked himself, seeing Porter taking out his soldiers.

Porter moved with such strength that even R'akl's own soldiers began to move themselves from his path as he continued taking out Ivo's soldiers.

"Do you sense something strange with Porter?" R'akl asked Lola.

"He seems different. More strengthened than before."

Their armor ripped from the chain-blade as he impaled them. Others he managed to decapitate with his sword. Porter had become something else during the battle. Porter had managed to takeout a large number of soldiers and found his way in front of Ivo.

"You didn't take the leave." Porter said.

"I… I do not fear you, Earthman. Whatever you've done to yourself, it will not be enough to defeat me."

Ivo raised his sword against Porter's. A smile formed on Mark's face as he whipped the blade from Ivo's hand with the chain-blade and held his sword with a straightened fashion as the tip was near toward Ivo's neck. Rankez froze from the sight, unable to reach down for his weapon.

"You have a decision to make." Porter said. "Surrender and go or die by my sword."

Ivo looked up once again toward R'akl and saw nothing upon his face. No expression of a helping hand. His breathing increased in concern and Porter remained still. His sword not moved. The anger within him began to boil and with a loud scream as he saw most of his soldiers dead by Porter's own hands.

"Enough!"

Ivo went for a strike, Porter moved, swiping his sword and slashing Ivo's right thigh. Falling to the ground on one knee, Porter placed his sword over Ivo's head as he glared up to the sun's glinting light upon the steel.

"Death is what you want?"

"It will be all I take."

"Hold still!" R'akl yelled behind Porter.

Moving his sword as he stepped back, R'akl approached the wounded Ivo and sighed with bitter.

"You will not meet your death today, Rankez. We allow you to leave Taranopolis only to give Saban Jai a warning. Never think of trying this again. Otherwise, you will both meet your end."

Ivo sighed with a hint of pain in his voice. Moving through his breath.

"You will regret this." Ivo said. "Mark my words."

Ivo turned away and fled into the desert. Once he was out of their sights, the city celebrated their victory with them cheering Porter's name. during the festivities, R'akl and Lola approached Porter, who stood atop the balcony, looking down at the civilians and nodded to their cheers.

"Porter." Lola said. "Me and my father wish to speak with you."

"What is it?"

"You did well on the battlefield today." R'akl said. "However, we couldn't help but notice your strength. How strong you've become since you've dwelt upon this planet."

"Your focus was stronger than I saw back at the arena." Lola said. "You seemed determined."

"I will admit. The atmosphere of this planet. It has changed me. My strength has increased. I can lift objects that weigh far beyond my capabilities on Earth. It's as I've become superhuman. As humans on Earth would say."

"Your hair has even grown longer than before." R'akl pointed. "I didn't even notice until now."

"Do you believe Ivo will return with Saban and more soldiers?"

"He will." Lola said. "Saban is only delaying his attack. Better we find him before he strikes us."

"Indeed." R'akl answered. "Yet, there is the other matter you two must attend to. Omnicron."

Porter nodded.

"Where do we start?"

"We'll head to the main library of the city. Your friend from the arena operates there now."

"You speak of Nakir?"

"I do. He often talks of your actions in the arena."

"Best we go to meet him."

Sometime later, Ivo still wandered in the desert. He had lost his tracks and begun to wander. Only seeing the vastness of the sands in front and around him. The pain continued in his leg as he fell to the sands. Breathing from tiredness and dehydrated, vo pondered his death.

"What are you doing out here alone?" said a voice in front of Ivo.

"What? Who's there?" Ivo asked, raising his head.

Ivo looked and with a glare, he only saw a figure standing before him. Dressed in brightly-keen white. Their eyes as blue as the seas of Earth. Ivo didn't know what to make of the stranger, yet he felt a unsettling energy from his presence.

"Do not fear me, Ivo Rankez. I am here to help."

"How do you know my name?"

"I know much on this planet. So much."

"And who are you?"

"I am a God of Argoron."

Ivo's eyes widen.

"A god of Argoron?!"

"Indeed. Now, shall I assist you back to your camp?"

Ivo paused. Unsure of what to do next. A small thought passed before his mind and he sighed.

"Please."

CHAPTER 4: A WONDER TO GAZE UPON A GOD

Ivo made his return to the camp, seeing the reaction from the soldiers standing in concern. Upon his return, the soldiers spotted Omnicron following him. As he entered the boundaries of the camp, the soldiers became instilled with fear. Omnicron paused in his steps, facing the soldiers. He raised his right hand and nodded.

"There is no need to fear me. I am here to offer help in your aid."

The soldiers remained still as Omnicron's presence moved past them. Ivo entered the main tent where Saban stood over the map. His eyes looked up, seeing his lieutenant. Ivo was tired and stumbled at the entrance. Saban commanded the two soldiers at the entrance to grab Ivo and place him in the nearby chair to the side of the entrance. Once they did, Omnicron stood at the entrance to Saban's surprise.

"Ivo. Who is this man?"

"He's not a man." Ivo answered slowly. "He's... he's a god."

"A god? A god of what?"

"There is no need to concern yourself, Saban Jai."

"How do you know my name?"

"As Ivo Rankez has told you. I am a god. A god of Argoron."

Saban nodded slowly as he stepped away from the map. He

moved closer toward Omnicron and stood to face him. Measuring him as his hand was placed upon the handle of his sword.

"How can I be certain you're telling me the truth?"

"I will show you."

Omnicron entered the tent and approached Ivo. Seeing him tired and dehydrated, Omnicron moved closer, placing his palm over Ivo's forehead and within seconds, Ivo was refreshed. He was well and lifted himself up from the chair. No longer slouching to the sides. The soldiers who saw it began to gasp as they stepped away from the tent with their hands on their weapons. Omnicron smiled toward Ivo.

"You are healed."

"Ivo." Saban said. "How do you feel?"

"I feel much better now. Completely restored."

Saban could tell Ivo was healed. In a way, Ivo stood up from the chair and moved with a force he hasn't had in years. It was almost as if Omicron managed to improve not only Ivo's tiredness and dehydration, but he had restored the strength he once had in his youth. Something Ivo had wished for continuously to himself.

"Is that enough to prove my honesty toward you?"

Saban gave Omnicron a nod of respect.

"It does." Saban answered, returning to the map. "Tell me why you followed Ivo here?"

"To bring him to safety to start."

"And what kind of god are you?"

"A god who grants the desires of those in need. Whether to restore their health or to gain them victory over their enemies."

The eyes of Saban sharpened greatly. Such words he wished to hear.

"Enemies? You can assist those in war?"

"I can."

"Perhaps you can help me. Since you've help my lieutenant in his health, I ask of a favor. One of a great importance."

"What is this you seek?"

"I am preparing for a war against King R'akl of Taranopolis. His kingdom is rightfully mine as is his daughter, the Princess Lola Arribel. However, our last encounter did not end well on my part. We were defeated."

"By the Earthman? Correct."

"Yes. How did you know?"

"After your battle, I came to him. Offered him something he needs while on this planet. A foreigner he is when he stumbles across the bloodlust sands."

"He is my enemy."

"That I know. What do you seek to do with him?"

"I will kill him once I deal with the King and his daughter."

"And you desire to rule Taranopolis and claim the kingdom for yourself?"

"I do."

Omnicron grinned, extending his hand toward one of the other chairs in the tent.

"May I?"

"Sure."

Omnicron sat and Saban sat with him as he began to ask more questions concerning Omnicron's power and his desire for Taranopolis. Omnicron craved every word which Saban spoke. From his plans of invasion to the takeover of the kingdom and eventually, the conquest of the entire planet.

Meanwhile in the city of Taranopolis, Porter and Lola made their entry into the main library of the city. A vast place within the middle of the city. Its structure reminded Porter of the ancient libraries of the past. To him, the library was designed in similarity to ancient Greek locations. Marble floors and limestone pillars. Inside, Porter was astonished by the amount of civilians who walked throughout the library. Each carried either scrolls or books. Several sat at the tables in the center of the halls, reading.

"I can take it you're surprised by all of this." Lola said.

"I am. Didn't know there was a place like this here. It, it reminds me of some places back on Earth."

"Do they libraries this size?"

"Some. Although the structure here would be considered ancient back on Earth."

As they walked through the library, Lola spotted a dark-blue robed man, removing himself from a ladder to reach a higher shelf. Once his feet touched the floor, he turned around in their sights. Porter looked and saw him. Nodding.

"Nakir." Porter said.

"He came here to be of service. It's what he said he wished for."

Porter walked over toward him and to Nakir's surprise. He looked up from the scrolls in his hands and saw him. A smile grew on his face and they embraced in a brotherly hug. Nakir laughed out his joy of seeing Porter once again.

"I didn't expect you to be here in Taranopolis." Porter said. "I see your robes have been restored. More sapphire to the eyes."

"It was something the King had insisted in doing. Other than that I can say the same about you. You're still here. I figured you would've went back home."

"I tried. But, something called for me to remain here for a while. I am in need of this planet and I wish to help."

Nakir nodded with a grin.

"I knew you were a hero. A true one at best."

Nakir walked toward one of the empty tables, sitting the scrolls down.

"So, what brings you and the Princess to the library this day?"

"We're searching for knowledge concerning the gods of this planet."

"The gods of this planet?" Nakir answered. "What's going on?"

"Porter was visited by a god of Argoron. We discovered his name to be Omnicron."

"Omnicron? You're serious?"

"We are."

"And by the two of you being here, you know what Omnicron is and what he's capable of?"

"We're aware." Porter said. "That's why we need to find some insight on him and these other gods. In case they arrive."

"I understand. Follow me."

Porter and Lola followed Nakir toward a small section of the library. At the top of the section rested over the shelves within the wall. Sculpted and etched in. Porter saw it and was unable to read it due to it being in Argoronian. He pointed toward it, getting Lola's attention.

"What does that say?"

"*Em'Prach*." Lola answered. "The section of faiths."

"Like religions." Porter said. "Knowledge of worship."

"Exactly. So, you're familiar with such things."

"I am."

Nakir moved across the shelves, searching through the scrolls as there were no books in the section. The scrolls were much older than anything else within the library. Dust covered the shelves and parts of several scrolls were torn. Worn out due to weathering and time. Nakir grabbed one of the scrolls and opened it, he turned toward Porter and Lola.

"What have you found?" Lola asked.

"This scrolls details the ancient past of warfare of this planet. All caused by Omnicron. The ancient kingdoms of the past were tricked by his ways. He manipulated the kings in conflicts with one another. Bringing much bloodshed to the planet. After he was caught, the other gods banished him from ever interacting with

Argoronians again. I guess that's changed now hasn't it."

"Porter isn't native to this planet." Lola said. "Perhaps that's why he revealed himself to you."

"Possibly." Porter replied. "We can't be certain of that."

"True." Lola said. "Anything else?"

"That's all it details. Are you going to try and find him again?"

"No." Porter said. "We're going to bring him out in the open."

Lola paused as did Nakir.

"And how are we going to do that?" Lola questioned. "He's a god. He doesn't appear as us in similar form."

"There has to be a way to bring him out into the open. From what Nakir read to us, the gods were visibly seen back in the ancient days. The same can be brought forth now."

"What Porter speaks is true, Princess." Nakir said. "I'm certain there is a way. I've read something about it when I began working here."

Nakir approached another shelf in the same location. Reaching up toward the third shelf, Nakir opened the scrolls. Showing Porter and Lola. Upon the scroll was drawn an object with only a few words written over and under it.

"What is that?" Lola asked.

"It's an orb." Porter said.

"Correct." Nakir replied. "It is said this orb has the power to bring forth a god of Argoron into the physical world. Any god of Argoron. All one must do is speak their name."

Porter nodded.

"Where do we find this orb?"

"Wait. You can't just be sure it will work."

"Lola, this is the only choice we have. We find this orb and we bring Omnicron out into the light. End all of this."

"The orb is kept hidden deep within the Hibrarian Forest."

"The Hibrarian Forest." Porter said. "I've heard it before."

"Yeah. When we were in the arena. Those Plant Men you fought, they're from that forest. It's their home."

Porter nodded. He asked for the scroll with Nakir declining. Surprising him and Lola.

"Why not?"

"Because I'm going along."

"Nakir, are you certain you want to be out there?" Porter asked. "Surrounding by enemies from all corners?"

"You're going out there to retrieve something that's claimed to be only a legend. I'm tagging along."

Porter understood.

"We'll need one more member for this adventure." Lola said.

"Who do you have in mind?" Porter questioned.

"We'll need to go to Alderan."

"Alderan?" Nakir said. "Why Alderan?"

"Because it was taken over by the Celedians after Porter killed the Wyvern King. Remember?"

"You're right."

"Then let's go to Alderan." Porter nodded.

The three took their leave from Taranopolis and traveled through the desert toward Alderan using ground travellers for a much faster pace. To their knowledge, the last time they saw the city, it was surrounded by wyvern men flying through the skies with wyverns themselves. The city smelt of blood and decay. Now, it is blooming with flowers. Green roses were present at the gates. The scent in the air was now reminiscent of cinnamon to Porter.

"This place has changed greatly." Nakir said. "I wonder what else has changed."

The gates of the city opened and as they entered, they saw a city flowing with Celedians. Families and children moving though the streets. The marketplace was crowded with many Celedians buying and selling.

"Such a place I've never seen." Porter said.

"Best we make it to the palace. I know he's inside."

"You're speaking of Tartarus Kai?"

"I am. We'll need his help on this."

Nearing the palace, they stepped from the traveller and walked up the stairs toward the palace doors. Seeing the structure surrounded with Celedian soldiers. All armed with spears. The doors opened and sitting on the throne was Tartarus himself. Seeing the three enter, he stood up and greeted them like family.

"What brings you three to our city?"

"We're on a mission." Porter said. "Heading into the Hibarian Forest to find an ancient object."

"A treasure hunt? Intriguing. What is all of this for?"

"We're trying to bring a god into our physical plane." Lola answered.

"A god? Which god?"

"Omnicron." Nakir said quietly.

"The God of Destruction." Tartarus replied. "And why would you do such a thing?"

"He appeared to me after the victory over Saban Jai." Porter said. "He's about to bring chaos to the planet and we're trying to stop him."

"And this object you're searching for in the forest? You'll need some assistance getting through there?"

"That's why we've come to you. Figured it would be best to gain some of your soldiers to aid us in this endeavor." Lola answered.

"Soldiers?! Ha. I'm coming too."

"You are?" Porter said. "Why?"

"Because this is a one-in-a-lifetime opportunity. Who can ever say they've fought against a god of destruction other than the ancients?"

Porter nodded as he saw several soldiers standing guard at the doors. They saluted toward Tartarus, ensuring their involvement with the quest. Tartarus left the throne and walked toward the doors. He turned toward them, wielding his own spear and sword.

"Let's go to the Hibarian Forest."

CHAPTER 5: THE HIBARIAN FOREST

With over a dozen Celedian soldiers behind them, Porter, Lola, Nakir, and Tartarus made their arrival at the Hibarian Forest. Miles away from Taranopolis and Alderan combined. Porter was astonished by the tall trees which stood before him in the midst of the desert. The red sands quickly turned into fields of emerald grass within a distance.

"Wasn't aware this planet had so much grass." Porter pointed.

"This is one of the only places on the planet which has a landscape like this." Tartarus said. "The forest itself keeps the ground alive. It is why it's far from civilization. To keep the balance."

"You mean there are other forests on this planet."

"Several. Each one is different than the other. Some are warm. Others are cold."

"That's different." Porter replied. "Now, do we proceed or what?"

"Prepare your arms." Tartarus said, gripping his spear. "Once we're inside, there's no telling when these Plant Men will strike. Among the beasts in this forest."

"I'm ready." Porter answered, wielding the chain-blade in his left hand.

The group was ready and they entered the forest. Completely being shaded by the trees from the sun's rays. Within the forest, the sounds of chirping echoed, surprising Porter as the wind moved through the tree line, blowing past them.

This place is very different." Porter noted.

"Aye." Tartarus replied. "This forest is one of many diversions. It can be peaceful or deadly."

While they walked, moving past bushes which stood nearly at the same height as the tall palm trees, the ground shook. They stopped in their steps as Porter looked at their surroundings. Seeing nothing but the trees. Taking notice they continued to move forward as the ground shook once more.

"What is that?" Nakir questioned.

"Earthquake?" Porter said.

"You mean a *Mintremor*." Lola said.

"Is that what they're called here?"

"It is. Earthquake is on the nose to where you're from."

The tremors beneath their feet continued and grew in strength. Almost to the point of increasing their position. Tartarus raised up his spear. His eyes moved across the tree line, facing another position. Staring deep into the trees ahead.

"Tartarus?" Porter said. "What is it?"

"We're not alone."

The tremors grew in location and sound. Tartarus told the others to prepare and from the trees bolted out giants. Standing nearly at the height of the trees. Their tall structure brought fear upon Nakir. Lola stepped back as Tartarus and Porter moved forward. Each with their weapons ready.

"Giants?" Porter said.

"Yes. They're native to this forest. It is their home."

The giants, covered in skins from their waist down. The feet bare and in their hands they welded clubs made from the stones of the ground mixed with the bark of the forest' trees. Three of them stood before the group and the first one glared down, seeing them.

"They're onto us." Nakir said.

"We know." Porter said. "What's the plan?"

"We attack only if they strike first." Tartarus said.

The giant knelt down to gain a better view of them. Its eyes the same shade as Coppertone. Its breath smelt of the forest and its voice rolled in its throat like a bellowing thunder. The giant rose up and looked at the others. Giving them a nod.

"What are they saying?" Porter questioned.

"Get your sword ready." Tartarus answered. "The fight is about to begin."

The giants raised up their clubs and let out a sharpening roar. Lola and Nakir covered their rears from the rushing sound as Porter and Tartarus yelled back, rushing to the giants with their weapons. Tartarus took his spear and swiped the leg of the first giant as Porter used the chain-blade to slash against the other two giants. The giants were not bothered as they moved the clubs and dragged them across the ground. Porter and Tartarus leaped from the incoming attacks.

"There aren't so bad." Porter grinned.

"You're sounding like a madman."

"Only a madman would face giants like these head-on."

Porter ran toward the three giants with his chain-blade and sword. Through the air, Porter slashed away with the blade as he took his sword and impaled the first giant in its chest. The giant fell onto the ground as Porter continued his attack on the other two giants. He moved with such speed, it resembled the battle in Taranopolis to Lola. Tartarus stood by watching the fight. Nakir was uncertain what to make of Porter's actions.

"What's happened with him?"

"His time here has changed him." Lola said. "In a way."

The second giants went for a strike, only for Porter to duck from the incoming club strike and swung the chain-blade across the throat of the giant. Grabbing itself quickly to avoid the blood flow, Porter grinned as the giant crouched to the ground, crawling away. The third and final giant did not turn back and stood firm. Slamming its club into the dirt.

"Very well." Porter said.

Porter nodded with a smile and ran toward the tall figure, twirling the chain and holding his sword. Porter leaped into the air as the blade swung forward, striking the giant in its chest. Porter held his sword with both hands and sliced the abdomen of the giant. To the point of bursting through the tough skin. Porter landed on the ground as the giant behind him fell to its death. Blood moved through the grass like a flood.

"What was that?" Tartarus questioned.

"They sought a battle." Porter answered. "We proceeded and ended it."

Porter sheathed his sword and moved the blade to his side while wrapping the chain around his left forearm. He nodded. Nakir was somewhat fearful of Porter's newfound strength.

"Best we get moving." Tartarus said. "Avoid more trouble."

Continuing their walk through the forest. Porter and Tartarus stood in front as Lola and Nakir remained in the back, watching their sights. No sign of any plant men to their surprise. Tartarus believed they were hibernating while Porter suggested they're hidden amongst the trees and the bushes. Invisible to their eyes. The sound around them became still. Even the birds in the air were silenced. Porter stopped and pointed towards something ahead.

"What is it?" Tartarus asked.

"There's something there. Past these trees."

Porter went ahead and moved through the bushes, swiping them down with his sword. Reaching the last bush, Porter sliced and saw himself standing in front of a massive structure. Tartarus, Lola, and Nakir came out of the tree line and stood in awe of the structure. To Porter, it reminded him of Mayan temples. Nearly standing over 40 stories, the structure was cleaner than the forest. There was no grass around the structure and the trees gave it shade aside from the center.

"I had no idea these were still around." Tartarus said. "Never one which stood perfectly structured."

"What are these?" Porter questioned. "I've seen similar structures back on Earth. They're ancient to us."

"These are the Temples of the Kadhai." Nakir said. "They belonged to a tribe which once was the most powerful across Argoron."

"What happened to them?" Porter asked.

"They were killed." Lola said. "A great war. My father told me about it when I was a child."

Porter stepped forward until another tremble shook the ground. Pausing himself as another tremor occurred. However, these were stronger than the ones created by the giants. Tartarus could sense something bigger was coming. They readied themselves for a possible fight and from the other end of the temple appeared a large beast. Colossal in nature. In Porter's eyes, it appeared as an albino elephant. Its four tusks were golden. There was something emerald around its neck like a necklace made for the animal. Tartarus moved closer to the trees as he fully saw the animal. He fell to his knees.

"No." Tartarus whispered.

"What is it?" Porter asked.

"They exist." Nakir said.

"What exists?"

"The Airavat." Lola answered still.

The Airavat walked toward them. Its golden eyes locked on them like a hunter. Lola and Nakir stepped back while Tartarus remained kneeling. Only Porter stood firm and even took a step forward.

"Mark Porter of Earth!" Lola yelled. "What are you doing?"

"Making myself known to the beast."

Porter sheeted his sword as the Airavat approached him. The beast was the same height as the temple and lowered its head to gain a better view of the Earthman. The low breathing of the animal rumbled the ground. Tartarus raised his head to see what was happening. Lola and Nakir watched on from the trees.

"What is he doing?" Tartarus questioned.

Porter and the Airavat locked eyes. For several minutes, they stared into each other's souls. Sensing a similar energy. Porter closed his eyes and nodded toward the animal and the Airavat did the same before turning aside.

"He's granted you passage." Tartarus said, watching it transpire.

"We can enter the temple." Porter said. "There's something inside."

"How are you certain of that?" Lola wondered.

"The Airavat told me."

With the animal to the side, they entered the stone temple. Within was air which seemed filtered unlike the outside. The interior covered with art of the Kadhai culture. Porter still said it reminded him of ancient Mayan artwork.

"If I may ask." Porter said. "What was this structure for? Its purpose amongst the Kadhai?"

"They used these temples for worship." Tartarus answered.

"To their gods. As it is everywhere."

"The map said it should be here." Nakir mentioned, taking out the map for a double check.

"Then, where would they place such a valuable object?" Lola questioned. "The throne room?"

"There's no throne in this building." Porter said. "Unless one of their gods physically entered this place."

Porter paused himself and turned to Tartarus.

"There's a throne room in this place, isn't there?"

"They never called it a throne. Only a place of worship."

"Like a tabernacle?" Porter said.

"Exactly." Nakir pointed as he moved down the corridor of the temple. Finding it taking them to a much greater room. Upon coming to its doors. The darkness was too great for them to see. A source of light was needed. Porter went back outside to gather branches to make a torch. While outside, he glared up to the top of the temple and noticed the sunlight beaming down the center. For a moment he thought and returned to the group.

"The sunlight. It has to beam down in this room."

"Where?" Tartarus asked. "Where is the sunlight?"

"I'll be back." Porter said, returning to the outside.

Porter took another look at the temple as the Airavat walked around the structure. Porter leaped atop the temple like a simple jump and approached the centerpiece of the structure. Finding it sealed shut.

"No problem." Porter said, grabbing the hold of the centerpiece.

With his newfound strength, Porter managed to remove the cap as the sunlight entered the tabernacle like lightning, brightening up the entire room. The light moved throughout the tabernacle before striking itself onto an object sitting in the center of the room surrounded by four tall statues of Kadhai gods. Made of a mixture between steel and stone. Somewhat in similar fashion to the temple itself.

"My gods." Tartarus said.

"Look at this place." Nakir noticed, pointing gat the statues and the wall art.

"How old is this?" Lola wondered.

"Centuries old." Tartarus answered.

Porter returned inside the room as the group stared at the object. He pointed without haste toward the golden object sitting on a pillar of stone.

"It's the orb."

"Indeed it is." Nakir said, approaching the object.

"This is how they were able to see their gods." Tartarus said. "That is why they worshiped them with such honor and integrity."

"Let's take what we came for and make our way back to Taranopolis." Porter said. "Bring forth Omnicron and finish this."

"You know, once we take this, the plant men will be onto us." Tartarus said.

"Let them try and stop us." Porter grinned.

Nakir grabbed the object and without haste, the statues of the Kadhai gods awoke. Their eyes beamed golden rays as they lifted up their steel swords, swiping and slashing at the four strangers in the temple. Porter raised his own sword and clashed with one of the statues. Tartarus and Lola took on the other two and the fourth stalked Nakir toward the exit. Porter quickie moved, stumbling the statue before decapitating it. Tartarus grabbed the other statue and ripped its arms apart with his own strength as Lola managed to slice the leg of the statue she was fighting. Porter rushed over and aided Nakir as the historian kicked the statue into Porter's sword. With a grin, he tossed the statue into the air, throwing his blade into the chest of the statue and pulling it back down with his chain-blade to the temple floor, shattering it into pieces. With a moment like it had passed, the group agreed and they made their exit.

CHAPTER 6: THE WAY FORWARD

Running back toward their travellers, rustling shook the trees above them. They did not hesitate or pause to grab a look. They continued moving and as they did, Plant Men pounced from the top of the trees onto the ground, chasing the three. While making their escape, on their left side, a herd of foreign ground travellers bolted through the bushes and trees. Upon them were Saban, Ivo, and his soldiers. Porter stopped and stared at Saban, who grinned.

"Saban Jai." Tartarus said.

"Don't give him any thought." Lola suggested. "We need to keep moving."

"Did you think you wouldn't see me again?!" Saban yelled. "Mark Porter of Earth!"

Porter looked and glared toward Saban. With a grin on his face, Porter grabbed his sword, slowly lifting it from its sheath on his back. Lola stepped in front, staring into his eyes as he was fixated on Saban.

"Porter, we need to go now." Lola continued to say.

"I know." Porter softly replied. "However, Saban cannot get away. Not this time."

"You'll get him next time." Tartarus pointed. "Right now, we need t focus on this orb. Bring out Omnicron."

Porter raised up his sword, pointing it toward Saban who laughed in reply. The group moved as Saban's forces were ambushed by he plant men. Entering a conflict with them, the ground trembled once again. Although this time it wasn't from giants. On the backend of the forest where the three came through, another creature rammed through the trees, knocking them down. Saban looked up as he saw the creature in full as it roared at him and his men.

"A Ruin Beast."

The gruesome creature with hide as dark as shadows. Eyes drawn blood-red. The Ruin Beast began attacking both Saban's forces and the plant men. Tartarus heard the roar of the creature and sped up in his movement as he is aware of the nature of the Ruin Beast. Seeing this as a no-win situation, Saban rallied Ivo and his remaining men to make their escape from the forest and follow Porter. On the outside of the forest, Porter, Lola, Tartarus, and Nakir made their exist as they leaped into their travellers and fled the area. Several minutes after, Saban and his soldiers exited and saw no sigh of Porter.

"Ugh." Saban sighed. "I was this close. This close to stopping him."

"There is still time." Omnicron said, appearing from in front of Saban like a blast of light.

"How are you certain?"

"He's in the possession of something which des not belong to him."

"What did he take?"

"A tool of the gods. Now, because of this current circumstance, you'll need to take it from him."

"Will you still aid me in taking over Taranopolis and this planet?"

"Retrieving the object from the Earthmen shall grant you such abilities. Abilities one like yourself could not fathom."

"Where have they gone?" Saban questioned.

"They are returning to Taranopolis as we speak. They intend on using the object without haste. You must be ready for I am ready."

Saban nodded in agreement and looked back at his soldiers. Seeing them in fear of the Ruin Beast and the plant men attacks. He knew they needed a small break and returned to his camp. There, he and Ivo spoke with Omicron concerning the object and the value of it. Saban remained in his tent in deep thought from then on.

The dead bodies of Saban's soldiers and plant men remained on the ground. Several were taken by the Ruin Beast as food, leaving the remaining ones became food for the Turuls which descended from the sky in the quietness of the dusk.

Back in Taranopolis, Porter remained in his chambers staring at the orb. Sitting still in his chair. His hand caressing his beard. Behind him, Lola entered and stood beside him. Comforting him as he focused.

"What's next?" Lola questioned.

"We wait till the morning. Summon Omnicron before all of us and end his plans for destruction."

"And then? What of Saban and his forces? We know they'll surely make themselves known during this."

"Then?" Porter nodded. "We will have the victory."

CHAPTER 7: SUMMONING THE GOD

The following morning, Porter prepared himself within the armory. Lola stood beside him as she assisted in his gear. They both knew once the orb was activated, Omnicron would come for a fight. Yet, how does one fight a god? Porter thought of such a question and did not succumb to the fear it presented within him. Lola placed on Porter's forearm gauntlets, his armored knee pads. Porter donned his new bronze armor torso piece. Detailed with Argoronian writings. Porter grabbed his chain-blade from the wall where it was hung. He twirled the blade with a nod as he rolled the chain on his left forearm and placed the blade atop his forearm. Lola approached the right wall and presented Porter with a shield.

"Where'd you get that?"

"It was something I had made for you." Lola smiled.

"I'm honored."

Porter took hold of the shield. Measuring its weight and he approved of such a gift. Last, Lola brought Porter one of the Argoronian helmets he looked down toward it with a faint grin and nodded.

"I have no need for a helmet."

"Are you sure?"

"I'll be fine."

"Wait." Lola said. "There's one more thing."

"I have what I need."

"Not all."

Lola opened the closet door and pulled out a cape. One darker than the red sands of the planet. She gave Porter a look of gesture to which he smiled and held out his hand.

"Let me see."

Handing him the cape, Porter felt its texture and even swung it around the room to see its weight amongst the air. He chuckled with a smile.

"What's funny?" Lola asked.

"Nothing. Nothing at all. This is nice. Thank you."

The army of Taranopolis stood outside the palace walls. Facing the entrance to the city. King R'akl stood with them in front. In the distance, they could see an incoming army. One they knew was Saban's own forces. Behind the army and the King arrived Porter and Lola. The soldiers were amazed by Porter's newfound attire. The armor shined like the fine gold and his cape moved smoothly in the air. Nakir arrived at the scene with the orb in hand.

"Are we sure we want to do this?" Nakir asked.

"It's the only way to end this." Porter said, taking the orb. "Now, what must I do?"

"You have to just call him out."

"That's all? No proper lines of words. Simply call him by name?"

"That's what the texts said."

Porter nodded as he held the orb in his right hand. Extending his arm. As Porter began to speak, Saban's forces had arrived at the entrance and they stopped. As if they were waiting. R'akl was confused about their motives as Porter noticed the orb glowing.

"I call you out. Omnicron. Come forth before us all."

The desert winds increased in their strength. Startling the soldiers and the civilians who began to return to their homes. Porter and Lola stood firm. R'akl held his sword tightly as he felt the winds across his face. Near the entrance, Saban's forces shielded themselves from the lifting sands. Saban peeked through his fingers and saw a beam of light in front of him. Standing in between his army and the city. The light manifested into three separate beings and once the light diminished, only Omnicron stood. On both sides were large beoths. Growling as they stared toward Porter, seeing the orb.

"There is he." R'akl said. "The God of Destruction."

Omnicron grinned as he took a look toward Taranopolis. Measuring his sights upon R'akl's army. He looked back toward Saban and gave him only a nod.

"You've summoned me into the material realm, Mark Porter of Earth."

Porter stepped forward, placing the orb into a pocket attached to his tunic.

"Whatever you have planned, it ends today."

"What I have planned? You insignificant speck of matter. What I have planned will bring forth live amongst all who dwell upon this planet."

The beoths continued to growl. Pouncing their eight legs within the sands beneath them. Omnicron could sense the fear upon R'akl's soldiers. He knew they had half a chance at victory. He petted the two beasts, calming them.

"You cannot win this battle, Omnicron." R'akl said. "We have many men on our side."

"It seems you've all forgotten I am a god. Whatever might you may possess in skill set doesn't match the power I possess."

"We will see." Porter said. "Won't we."

"If that is what you wish."

"Let's end this. Between your destruction upon this planet and while we're at it. Saban and his forces go down as well."

"Saban Jai. A skilled warrior. Brilliant tactician. Ah." Omnicron paused. "He didn't mention it to you did he?"

"Mention what?" Porter questioned.

"He's only here on my account."

Omnicron turned toward Saban, signaling him to walk forward. Saban stood beside Omnicron, looking down at the brute beoth.

"Don't fear the beast. He will not harm you. We're on the same side."

"I understand.." Saban replied, turning to see Porter. "Can I signal the attack?"

"Do it." Omnicron grinned. "Commence the war."

Saban smiled and gave a look toward his army. Ivo knew the look and raised up the banner of Jai. Once the winds touched it, the army let out a raging war cry. Omnicron raised his hands and the beoths went loose into the city with Saban's army behind them. R'akl signed his army to attack as he went forward. Lola followed her father into battle as did Porter. The armies came closer with Omnicron walking through Saban's forces like flowing mist. Porter's eyes were set on both Omnicron and Saban as the two locked in upon him. Saban reached for his sword with a smile on his face. Porter held his in-hand as his left hand let loose the chain and began twirling the blade.

"This is my victory!" Saban screamed.

"Yes!" Omnicron yelled. "YES!"

The armies ran and the beoths lunged into battle. The swords clashed and the blood spilled. The battle for Taranopolis had begun.

CHAPTER 8: BETWEEN GODS AND MEN

Blood spilled from the chaos that was the battle. R'akl slaughtered several of Saban's soldiers as Porter rushed through the crowd, slashing away with his sword and tossing his chain-blade. His eyes were set on reaching Saban and Omnicron. Quickly eliminating the last three soldiers in his path, Porter stood firm facing Saban and Omnicron.

"You wanted him." Omnicron said toward Saban.

"This is my chance." Saban replied. "To end this perfectly."

"I am ready when you are." Porter said, holding his sword steady.

Saban took a breathe and yelled greatly as he rushed to attack Porter. Porter moved from the incoming sword slash and retaliated with a sword attack of his own. Going for Saban's legs. Yet, Saban deflected the sword with his own before delivering a series of punches to Porter's face. Shaking the attacks off, Porter grinned as blood showed on his mouth. The chain-blade slipped down as Porter caught the chain. Saban's eyes went toward it and he raised up his sword as Porter twirled the chain and the blade flew across Saban's face. Impacting his sword, causing the blade to slice the right side of his face. Saban held his face, seeing the blood and before he could conjure a thought, Porter rushed him with a brute blow to the head with his fist, knocking him to the ground. Omnicron looked down at Saban and sighed, yet applauded.

"Good work. You are a skilled warrior. For an Earthman."

"Whatever you had planned, it ends this day."

"Does it? Very well. Allow me to show you what I have seen and what is to come."

Raising his hands high in the air, Omnicron brought up the ground where he and Porter stood, lifting into the sky as Porter saw the clouds passing them. He ran toward Omnicron, only to be knocked back by a serious blast of wind which emitted from Omnicron's left hand. Catching himself before he fell off the lifting soil, Porter threw his chain-blade into the flying ground and tossed himself into the air. Almost in a punching stance over Omnicron, attacking the god with his bare hands.

"Get off me!" Omnicron yelled. "You dare touch a god!"

The red sky of Argoron quickly became darkness as Porter looked around, seeing the stars.

"You've never been in a place like this before have you? To see the stars closely than those upon the soils of these worlds."

"Where are we?"

"High above Argoron. I thought Earthmen couldn't breathe in an atmosphere without your oxygen. It seems Argoron's own atmosphere has changed you. Made you immune to even what your fellow Earthmen cannot handle."

"This isn't about them." Porter said, holding his sword. "This is between you and me."

"Is that what your truly believe? That I am the ultimate enemy? You were the cape of a king, yet do not possess the wisdom of one."

"For the short time I've been on Argoron, you're the worst that's come my way."

"The Wyvern King didn't bring you such harm. How could he. You were only an entertainment piece to him. No different than a gladiator."

The sky intensified in colors. Galaxies appeared around them as did falling stars. Porter was amazed at what he saw. In the distance of the glistening colors of sapphire and emerald appeared planets. All unfamiliar to Porter.

"What is all of this?"

"The truth." Omnicron grinned. "These are worlds you've never known about. Worlds myself and my fellow brethren have managed to overlook. To watch."

"More Argoronian gods."

"There are gods everywhere, Mark Porter of Earth. We speak to one another at times."

"You're calling them to invade Argoron?"

"Not yet. Eventually."

"I cannot allow that to happen."

The chain-blade twirled as Porter threw it toward Omnicron. Before the god to manage a grab, the blade pulled back as Porter threw his sword instead. Rushing the blade through Omnicron's chest. Omnicron sighed as he pulled the sword from his body and tossed it back to Porter.

"You'll have to do more than impale me."

Omnicron raised his right hand as his eyes were set on Porter.

"Back down we go."

Lowering his right hand, the ground they stood on began to all back to Argoron. Moving past the stars once again before hitting the planet's atmosphere. Porter rushed toward Omicron with his sword. Going for any attack he could only for Omnicron to dodge the coming swipes. Omnicron pressed his left hand, shoving Porter back near the edge. Stopping his fall with his sword into the ground, Porter stood up and threw his sword with great strength, only for Omnicron to do the same with a sword of his own. The blades collided in the air, shaking the ground as they made impact onto Argoronian soil. Sand filled the air as Porter had fallen on his face. Raising his head, he could hear the continuing battle and he looked in front of him, seeing Omnicron standing, taunting him to rise up.

"This battle is not yet over." Omnicron said.

Porter stood up and grabbed his sword from the ground. Omnicron formed his own sword in his hand, made from material which Porter could only guess was crystal. The two ran toward each other, slamming their swords into one another as the shockwave moved throughout the battlefield. Omnicron's power was greater than Porter's newfound strength and he knew it. Omnicron grinned as he slammed his sword into Porter's once again, causing him to stumble.

"Brute force cannot defeat a god."

"I see. Then, there is another way. Something less deadly."

Porter arose, holding the orb in his hand. Omnicron saw the glow and went to reach for the object, Porter moved his chain across Omnicron's neck and commanded the god to return to his own realm. Unable to overtake the power of the orb, Omnicron vanished like a blast of smoke. With him gone, Saban's army became weakened and were defeated by R'akl's forces. The battle was over and the civilians celebrated the victory.

From there, Saban had vanished during the battle as did Omnicron's two beoths. Even Ivo had disappeared, only to be found in the desert a mere five days later captured by Celedians who brought him to Alderan. Taranopolis held a celebration feast for seven days. While the festivities took place, Porter remained inside the palace. Quiet. At the door walked in Lola who was concerned about Porter's state. She continued asking him of his circumstance, only to be told there was more to discover. More to learn.

When the seven days had ended, a mysterious event unfolded over the city. Snow began to fall. an omen to the Argoronians. Once they wore light clothing, now they're covered in much apparel. Even the skins and furs of the beasts across the wilds. R'akl met with Porter as he stepped out into the snowfall.

"What is happening?" Porter asked.

"I remember the tales." R'akl said. "Passed down through the generations."

"What is it?"

"The ancients have awoken. Omnicron was only the start of something worse. This is the end of Argoron as we know it."

Porter stood firm.

"As I live, it will not."

MARK PORTER WILL RETURN
IN

AVAILABLE NOW!

ABOUT THE AUTHOR

Ty'Ron W. C. Robinson II is the author of several works of fiction. Including the *Dark Titan Universe Saga, The Haunted City Saga, EverWar Universe, Symbolum Venatores, Frightened!, Instincts,* and others. More information pertaining to the author and stories can be found at darktitanentertainment.com.

Gettr: @TyronRobinsonII

Twitter: @DarkTitan_
Instagram: @darktitanentertainment
Facebook: @DarkTitanEnt
Pinterest: @darktitanentertainment
YouTube: Dark Titan Entertainment
Rumble: Dark Titan Entertainment

www.ingramcontent.com/pod-product-compliance
Lightning Source LLC
LaVergne TN
LVHW041556070526
838199LV00046B/2001